The Adventures of
HIGH JOHN
THE
CONQUEROR

THE ADVENTURES OF
HIGH JOHN
THE CONQUEROR

By Steve Sanfield

August House Publishers Inc.

LITTLE ROCK

Published by August House, Inc.
P.O. Box 3223, Little Rock, Arkansas 72203,
501-372-5450.

This book was made possible in part by a grant from
the Society of Children's Book Writers.

Reprinted by arrangement with Orchard Books.
Cover and interior illustrations by Wendell E. Hall.

Printed in the United States of America

10 9 8 7 6 5 4 3 2 1

LIBRARY OF CONGRESS CATALOGING-IN-PUBLICATION DATA

Sanfield, Steve.
The adventures of High John the Conqueror / Steve Sanfield ;
p.   cm.
Summary : A collection of sixteen tales about High John the Conqueror, the
traditional trickster hero of blacks during and immediately after
the time of slavery.
ISBN 0-87483-433-3
1. Afro-Americans—Folklore. 2. Tales—Southern States.
[1. Afro-Americans—Folklore. 2. Folklore—United States.]
I. Ward, John (John Clarence), ill. II. Title.
PZ8.1.S242Ad   1995
[398.2]—dc20 —dc 20
[398.22'08996073]   95-35825

The paper used in this publication meets the minimum requirements
of the American National Standards for Information Sciences—
permanence of Paper for Printed Library Materials, ANSI.48-1984

AUGUST HOUSE, INC.   PUBLISHERS   LITTLE ROCK

To the memory and spirit of
J. MASON BREWER
(1896–1975)
and
ZORA NEALE HURSTON
(1901–1960)
two of the first
to pass on the gift

Fool my master seven years.
Going to fool him seven more.
Hey diddle, de diddle, de diddle, de do.

attributed to Jake Green in
B. A. Bodkin's *Lay My Burden Down*

Contents

The Adventures of
HIGH JOHN
THE
CONQUEROR

Introduction

■ Do you ever have a bad day? Of course you do. Just about everyone does, and when one bad day follows another and another and still another, many of us start complaining about *hard times*.

But as difficult as these times might seem for you and me, there have been harder times, much harder times. I'm thinking of a time, as recent as 125 years ago, when that peculiar and horrible institution called slavery existed here in this country. Now those were hard times, especially if you were unfortunate enough to be counted among the almost four million men, women, and children who were slaves.

You didn't even own your body. Some other human being owned your body the same way we own a table or a tape recorder or an automobile, and they could do whatever they wanted with it. They could beat it. They could burn it. They could whip it. They could sell it. They could sell you from your mother, your children, your husband, your wife. They could tear your family apart, and there wasn't much you could do about it.

In more than two hundred years of slavery here, the slave owners tried to take everything away from the slaves: their homes, their family, their names, their language, their music, their religion, their dignity, their self-respect—*everything*.

In the eyes of the slaveholders, the slaves were less than human, but it's important to remember that to the slaves themselves, they were not slaves. They were people who lived under a condition called slavery, and what couldn't be taken away from them was the human spirit that even in times of the greatest adversity wills itself to, needs to go on living. It is this spirit that continues to speak for the very best in the human condition, to speak for life itself, and out of this spirit came a wondrous body of song and story.

Most of you are probably already familiar with some of those stories—stories about a little fellow who wasn't very big and wasn't very strong, but he was mighty quick and mighty smart, and folks called him Brer Rabbit.

The slaves often told stories about Brer Rabbit, about how, through his cunning and his tricks, he would overcome all the might and power and meanness of Brer Fox and Brer Bear and Brer Wolf. Whites would hear those stories and think, "Oh, isn't that cute, little Brer Rabbit fooling big Brer Bear." But when the slaves told and heard them, they heard them differently. They saw themselves as Brer Rabbit and the slaveholders as Brer Wolf and Brer Fox, and the only way to defeat all that power and brute force was to be just a little bit more clever.

But there was another group of stories that grew up in that time which white people never heard, and they never heard them because they weren't supposed to hear them. Those stories were about a man named John or High John or High John the Conqueror.

It's said that High John came across the water from Africa. Some people remember him as a big man. Others remember him as a small man. I myself don't rightly know, but I do know he was a *Be-Man.* He *be* there when the trouble come, and he *be* there when the trouble go.

Even though John was a slave, he hated slaving and loved living, and he tried to do as much living and as little slaving as possible. I mean, he'd pick up a shovel, and the shovel would break—accidentally, of course. He'd go out to the tool shed, and the tool shed would burn down—accidentally, of course. If he ever did get to the fields with the mules, the mules would tromp down four rows of cotton—accidentally, of course.

But some years he'd do the work of four or five men. When he picked cotton and was half trying, he could pick a thousand pounds a day, and when he was really trying, those cotton bolls flew so fast you would've thought you were in the middle of a blizzard.

Of course, Old Master could never quite figure out whether John was working for him or against him, and believe me, that's just the way John wanted it.

There he was playing his tricks, "making a way

out of no-way, hitting a straight lick with a crooked stick, winning the jackpot with no other stake but a laugh."*

As the old song says:

He wouldn't pick cotton and he wouldn't mow hay.
He wouldn't take a licking and he wouldn't run away.

And so, here is that hope-bringer, that will-to-dream, High John the Conqueror.

---

* Zora Neale Hurston, "High John the Conqueror," *The American Mercury Magazine*, October 1943.

Master's
Walking Stick

High John was, among other things, a fine fisherman. He knew where the fish lay, and he knew what had to be done to catch them.

Even Old Master liked to go fishing with John now and then. They'd go down to the big pond under the live oaks, and Master would try to catch a few catfish himself.

John and Master had planned to meet early one bright summer morning. John was already there behind the barn when along came Master. Of course he had his fishing pole with him, but he was also carrying a brand-new walking stick. The stick was polished almost as bright as a mirror. It had a shiny silver handle on one end and a shiny silver tip on the other.

From the way he was swinging and flashing it about, you could tell Master was very proud of his new stick. John, however, didn't make any mention of it, at least not until they were settled on the bank of the pond with their lines in the water.

"Say Massa," said John, "that's a mighty fine looking walking stick you've got there."

"Why thank you, John. I was beginning to wonder if you were going to take any notice of it."

"Oh Massa, I noticed it right off. I mean it's the only walking stick I've ever seen with three ends."

"Three ends?" asked Master. "What are you talking about, John?"

"Well, I ain't talking about anything but the three ends of that stick," John answered.

"John, are you drunk or have you gone crazy?"

"I'm not drunk and I'm not crazy, Massa, but I can see as clear as the nose on my face that your stick's got three ends."

"John, no stick's got three ends."

"Well, that one does," said John, "and I'd be willing to bet you a big, fat hen that it does."

Old Master took a careful look at his walking stick just to be sure. After all, John had been playing tricks on him for years. This time, though, he was certain John was wrong.

"Agreed," he said. "I'll bet you a hen that this stick has only two ends."

With that, John took the stick and held it out in front of him. He pointed to the silver handle and said, "That's one end, right?"

"Right," answered Master.

He pointed to the silver tip and said, "That's two ends, right?"

"Right," answered Master again.

Then John raised the stick over his head and threw it directly into the center of the pond, where it sank without a trace.

"And that's the third end of that stick, right?" said John with a twinkle in his eye.

Old Master didn't answer this time. He knew John had fooled him again, and that when they got back home he'd have to give him a nice plump hen.

Slaves were sold at auction, in much the same way as cattle or tobacco. The highest bidder would become the new owner, and although slaves cost a good deal of money—anywhere from a few hundred dollars for a young child to a few thousand for a field hand in his prime—many slave owners simply didn't take very good care of their "property."

They tried to get as much profit from their slaves at as little cost as possible, and often abused them in the process. Because a commonly held idea was, "They can take care of themselves," for the majority of the slaves there was a continuing shortage of food and clothing. Beyond the meager rations given to them by their owners, slaves often had to take what they needed to survive.

Whites called it stealing, but it wasn't stealing to the slaves. That's what you did when you took something from another slave. They knew that what they were taking from their owners was only what they, through their lives and labor and sweat, had made possible.

Just Possum

High John's favorite food in the whole world was roasted young pig. It also happened to be Old Master's favorite food, so except for Christmas and maybe a special day here and there, the slaves never got any.

John figured there wasn't any reason he shouldn't have pork whenever he wanted to, so he began to help himself. After dark he'd go to the pigpen, snatch up a piglet, and take it on down to his cabin. There he'd kill and dress his prize and cook himself up a fine meal.

Old Massa's got so many, he thought, *he won't even know they're gone.*

But John pilfered so many that Old Master soon began to notice their population was decreasing rapidly. He made up his mind to find out who the thief was and to give him a good thrashing.

Master took to sitting on the knoll above the pen, and one night, just as the moon was rising, who should he see coming around but High John himself. Master stayed out of sight and watched John scoop up one of the little pigs and take it on home.

This time he'd caught John in the act. No doubt about it. He didn't follow him right then, though. He wanted to be absolutely sure, so he went back to the Big House to allow John enough time to start cooking the piglet. The proof would be in the pot.

John seasoned it down good and put it in the big kettle hanging in the fireplace. He was sitting there dreaming about the pleasure ahead and chuckling to himself about how he'd got the best of Old Master again, when suddenly there was a knock on his door.

"Who's that?" John shouted, big and bold, never expecting it would be Master at the door.

"It's me, John," said Master, "and I want to come in."

"Oh no, Massa, that's all right. I'm coming out."

"John, I want to come in."

"Oh no, Massa, it wouldn't do for a gentleman like you to be seen in a little old slave cabin like this. Why I'd feel ashamed for you."

"No," Master insisted. "I'm coming in."

John couldn't do anything about it, and in came Master.

There wasn't much in the cabin: a bed of sorts made with pine poles and a mattress stuffed with wheat straw, a rickety table with two chairs made from bent willow, and in the fireplace a big black kettle bubbling away.

The pig had been cooking for a while and the air was filled with the sweet aroma of pork. John knew that Master could smell it and that he'd been caught good this time, but Master didn't say a single word about the pig. He just pulled up a chair and began to talk about the crops, the mules, the weather.

All the time there was the pig cooking away. The smell got richer and stronger, but Master kept on talking about this and that as if he hardly noticed. Finally, when the pig had just about simbled down to a fine gravy, Master asked, "What do you have cooking in that pot that smells so good?"

"Why Massa," said John, "that's just a little old possum I caught. Scrawniest little possum you ever did see, but I thought I'd cook it up anyway."

"Well, I think I'd like to try some," said Master.

"Oh Massa, a man like you don't want to eat no possum. Why you ain't even hungry."

"John, don't argue with me. I said I want to try some of that possum, and I want it now. If you don't serve it up right away, I'll have you whipped."

John didn't have much choice. He got a wooden bowl and a fork and went over to the kettle. Just as he was lifting the lid, he said, "Massa, when I put this thing in here it was a possum, but if it comes out a pig don't blame me."

Well, Old Master didn't want to laugh, but he couldn't help himself. He took the bowl and ate the pork, and all he said was, "This possum sure tastes good."

But from that time on, he made sure to let High John have a young pig for himself every now and then.

"You Better Not Do It"

■ Just about every plantation raised some kind of livestock, no matter what kind of crops it grew. It might be sheep or cows or goats or pigs or chickens. Old Master also used to raise a few turkeys so that he and his family could have a proper feast each Christmas and Thanksgiving. One year, however, the turkeys were scarce, and Master asked John to kill a sheep for the Thanksgiving dinner at the Big House.

John had never tasted mutton, but he thought, *If it's fine enough for Massa, then surely it's fine enough for me.* So before bringing the cleaned-out carcass to the kitchen, John cut off a good-sized chunk for himself.

He boiled it up in the iron kettle, and with the first bite he realized it was a tastier victual than any possum or hogback he'd ever had. Even before he'd finished it, John had a powerful craving for more. He tried to control it, knowing it could only lead to trouble, but when it came to his stomach, the important thing was to keep it full.

After a few weeks he convinced himself that he needed mutton the same way he needed water to live. Nothing else seemed to have that special taste. He didn't want to wait until next Thanksgiving, and it wasn't likely that Master was about to give him any, so John decided to take matters into his own hands.

One night, during the dark of the moon, he took an oak club and slipped on down to the sheep pen. He walked on his tiptoes, trying to be as quiet as a breath of air creeping through a crack, but just as he stepped into the pen, one of the sheep woke up. Without hesitation, John hit it square on its head and killed it.

Mmm, he thought, *if one's good, two are probably better.*

Just as he was about to hit another one, he heard footsteps approaching the pen. Even though it was dark and he couldn't see the person's face, he knew it was Old Master. After all, John's very life depended on knowing such things.

Master reached the gate, and John, holding the club high above his head, shouted as loudly as he could, "You better not do it! You better not do it! If any of you other sheep try to butt me like your brother just did, I'll have to kill you too."

With the slaves taking what they needed to survive, the overseers or foremen of the plantations began to miss things. One day the melon patch would be bursting with ripe fruit, but the next day much of it would be gone.

"What happened to the melons?" the overseers would ask.

The slaves would say, " 'Coons got 'em," meaning raccoons.

Then half the ripe ears of corn would be missing from the garden.

The overseers would ask, "What happened to the corn?"

" 'Coons got it," the slaves would say.

It didn't take the overseers very long to figure out just who was making off with the melons and the corn, and they began to refer to the slaves as "coons." Although the term later became a bitter racial slur, it was at first a begrudging recognition of cleverness and audacity.

In a Box

■ Knowledge can often mean power, and this is a truth High John came to understand early on. Usually the smartest slave on a plantation got the easiest work, so John was determined to prove to Old Master that he was the smartest of them all.

He took to sitting under the kitchen window at the Big House each evening just about the time Old Master and Missy were having their supper. He would sit there quietly and listen in the hope that he might learn something that would take a little of the slaving out of his life.

One spring evening he heard Master tell his wife, "Tomorrow I'm going to send John down to the bottomland and have him plow up that new ground."

John went back to his cabin, but the next morning he was up well before the sun. He got the plow out of the shed and the mules out of the barn and hitched them up. When Old Master came around and told him, "John, today I want you to plow the . . ." John cut him short and said, "Yes, I know, Massa. You want me to plow up that new ground. Well, I've got the mules hitched and I'm all ready to go."

"John, how did you know that's what I wanted you to do?" asked Master.

"Oh, I don't know how I knowed it but I do. I just seem to know everything."

John went down to the bottomland to do the plowing, and Master went on about his business without giving it any more thought. With cotton planting underway he had a good many other things on his mind.

That evening John sat under the kitchen window again and listened to Master talking to Missy. "It's time to clean out the stables. I think I'll have John do it and spread the manure on that new ground he plowed today."

When Master went to the stables the next morning, there was John raking out the bedding. He'd already cleaned two stalls.

"John," Master said, "how'd you know I wanted the stables cleaned out?"

"I told you, Massa. I know everything. I don't know how I know. I just do. Why there's probably nothing I can't foretell."

Old Master was a little puzzled by all this and said, "Something funny's going on around here."

"Maybe so," replied John, "but I do know things. When I get these stables cleaned out, I think I'll haul the dirty straw down to the new bottomland."

Master didn't say anything, but he began to consider that maybe John did have some special powers that let him know things.

Come evening, there was John under the window again, listening to Master making plans for the next day. "The barn leaked a lot during the last rains. I think I'll have John fix it."

Well, by the time Master got to the barn in the

morning, there was John carrying piles of wooden shakes up the ladder to the roof.

"John," he said, "you knew I wanted this roof fixed, didn't you?"

"I sure did, Massa. I sure did. I keep telling you I know everything and I can see everything. There ain't nothing hid from me."

John spent the day repairing the leaks, and Master rode off to a neighboring plantation to meet with the other farmers in those parts. After they talked about their crops and their problems with the slaves, Old Master began to brag about John.

"I've got a slave down on my place who seems to know everything. Every day when I go out to tell him what I want him to do, he's already doing it."

The others laughed at that. "You must be joking," one of them said. "There isn't a slave in the world who's that smart."

"I'm not joking," said Master. "My slave, John, *is* that smart. He knows everything, he sees everything, and you can't fool him."

"In all my days I've never known a slave I couldn't outsmart," boasted one of the men, and everyone else agreed with him.

"You can't outsmart John," shouted Master, who was getting angry about his word being questioned, "and furthermore, I'll bet on it."

There was more talk and more arguing, and before long Old Master ended up betting his whole plantation, his money, his slaves, just about everything he owned that his friends couldn't fool John.

"We'll come by your place tomorrow, and we'll have something your slave can't tell us about," they said.

Master felt so sure of his bet that he invited them all for a big party the next day. John had proved to him that he knew everything, and now John would show the others.

That evening as Master was telling his wife about what had happened, there sat John listening. "They'll all be coming over about noon, and I thought we'd put a nice spread out on the lawn."

John heard that and headed back to his own cabin. He figured that's all he needed to know.

And sure enough the next morning there was John setting up tables and chairs in front of the Big House.

"Ah, good for you, John," said Master when he came out. "You know we're going to have a grand party today, don't you?"

"I told you Massa, I know everything."

"That's good, because I made a very large bet on you."

"A bet on me?" asked John. "What kind of bet?"

"Come on," laughed Master. "You're just trying to fool me. I know you know everything, and that's just what I bet my friends."

John didn't say a word, because he didn't know what to say, but Master continued, "I bet all I own on you, John, and I'm depending on you. If you win then I'm going to make you a rich man, but if you don't then you're going to be one dead slave, because I'll whip every bit of skin off your body. You just be here when all my neighbors come."

John knew he was in trouble, but he didn't know what kind of trouble. *Maybe I've outsmarted myself this time,* he thought. He wanted to make himself scarce, but there was no way he could do that.

Before long, Master's friends and neighbors began to arrive. They brought their wives and children and some of their slaves too. They wanted everyone to see how they were going to make a fool out of John and his master.

Finally, when everyone had arrived, two of the

men took a large, wooden box from the back of one of the wagons and set it on the ground.

"You, John, come over here," one of them ordered.

John did as he was told, all the time wishing he were home sick in bed.

"We hear you're pretty smart," the man laughed.

"Oh, I wouldn't say that," John said softly.

"Well, your master says you are."

John couldn't very well argue with that, because it would certainly never do for a slave to contradict his owner in public.

"John," the man went on, "we've got a box here, and in that box is another box, and in that box is another box, and in that box is still another box, and in that box is something, and we want you to tell us what it is."

Old Master stepped forward and said, "Go ahead, John. Show them how you know everything. All you've got to do is tell them what's in that box, and you'll be a rich man. But if you don't, like I said, you're going to be one dead slave."

Now what they had put in that box in a box in a box in a box was a raccoon; and the reason they

put it in so many boxes was so John couldn't hear it scratching.

Everyone was so quiet that the loudest sounds were the tiny chickadees hopping from branch to branch in the magnolias overhead. Everyone was watching John, and John was watching the box. He stared at it harder and harder, but he didn't have the least idea what was in it. He scratched his head, and drops of sweat as big as your fist began pouring off him.

Sorrier than sorry that he'd ever tried to prove how smart he was, John began walking around the box trying to get an idea. "In a box, in a box, in a box, in a box," he mumbled as he circled it. "In a box, in a box, in a box, in a box. In a box, in a box, in a box, in a box."

He knew what kind of trouble he was in now, and he knew it was big trouble this time. He circled the box one more time. "In a box, in a box, in a box, in a box."

Finally he figured he might just as well give up. He turned to the crowd and said, "Well, you got the old coon at last."

Everyone started yelling with surprise, and when they turned all those boxes over a chubby raccoon ran out. Old Master threw his hat in the air and shouted, "I told you my John knew everything. I told you so."

And that's how Old Master won his bet and how High John became a rich man.

Off Limits

Whenever Old Master was feeling mean or angry or both, which could be pretty often, he would take it out on the slaves. That might mean a beating for anyone unfortunate enough to catch his eye. Or he might order the overseer to keep them working in the fields late into the night under the light of the full moon. Or worst of all, he might hold back on the meager rations given to the slaves, making their lives even more of a misery than they already were.

Sometimes, though, he could be just plain

pettifogging—like the time he announced that the catfish in the big pond were off limits to everyone except himself. From now on, he said, he was the only one who could catch them.

The slaves were still allowed to fish the pond once they'd completed their work or on Sundays when they weren't expected to labor, but if they hooked a catfish they had better throw it right back in the water where it came from. Otherwise, they'd be severely punished.

Oh, they were free to keep any other fish they caught, which was all well and good, except that the only other fish that lived in that pond were tiny perch not much bigger than a baby's hand. They were so small and so filled with bones like needles that they hardly seemed worth the trouble it took to clean and cook them.

After Master laid down his new law, John was the only one who kept right on fishing. Every Sunday he'd amble on down to the pond, set himself in the warm shade of the oaks and willows, and try his luck. When the others asked him why he bothered, he'd smile that big smile of his and say, "Oh, I just love them little perch. For me they're as sweet as sugar on the tongue."

The truth was that John didn't like the perch

any more than anyone else, but he certainly did like catfish, and it was catfish he was fishing for. He was bold enough to keep each and every one he pulled from the pond, and he was cagey enough to get them into his frying pan without anyone, including Master, seeing him do it.

Late one easy Sunday afternoon, John had fallen asleep in the long, dappled shadows and was dreaming his favorite dream about lying down and getting up when he wanted to, not when someone else thought he should. John was dreaming about freedom.

Just then, who should come walking by the pond but Old Master himself. He saw John napping, his pole in the water, a bunch of tiny perch in his bucket, and there, hanging on a string tied to the branch of a willow, a fat eight-pound catfish. He'd caught John just as sure as John had caught that catfish. No doubt about it.

He shook John awake, and the minute John opened his eyes and ears he didn't have any doubt about it either.

"Nice day," said Master, staring directly at that yellow and gray catfish gleaming in the sun. "How's the fishing today?"

John knew he was in the middle of a serious

devilment, and he was scared, but he had learned long ago that being scared didn't do anyone any good whatsoever unless that anyone was going to do something about it. He immediately began scrambling in his mind, thinking so hard you could almost hear the wheels spinning inside his head.

Meanwhile, Master was delighting in the situation and wanted to take as much pleasure from it as he could. He wanted to see John twist and turn just like a fish might do when it got itself hooked. "I asked you, John," he said slowly, "how's the fishing today?"

And that minute of playing with John was Master's mistake, because that was all the time John needed.

"You know, Massa," he said, "I've been having a terrible time today, a terrible time. Everything started out just fine. The perch were biting good. I had half a bucket before I was even settled in, and then this catfish heard I was here and began stealing my bait. I asked him to stop, but he kept right on taking it. Why, he wouldn't quit even when I ordered him to. Finally I had to catch him, Massa, or he would have stolen it all. But I'm done fishing now, so I guess I might as well turn him loose."

John untied the catfish and threw it back into the water where, with a single splash of its tail, it dove straight to the bottom of the pond. He picked up his pole and his bucket and started on home, leaving Old Master standing alone on the bank staring at the ripples the catfish made growing wider and wider and wider.

One of the most wonderful things about High John the Conqueror is that almost every story about him ends with a laugh. Despite all the hardships, John was just about unbeatable, and what let him win out over the whole mess of sorrow was that he could finish off almost any situation with a laugh. There are a number of tales about High John where the laugh's on him, but it's laughter nonetheless.

Laughter is strong medicine, maybe the most powerful medicine of all. It takes a great people and remarkable individuals to be able to laugh at themselves, especially in times of terrible adversity—but those who do usually manage to survive.

John Wins a Bet

Watermelons are as much a part of summer in the South as long, lazy days, and there wasn't a farm or a plantation that didn't have its own watermelon patch. When the melons were ripe, some farmers would fill their wagons with the big, green fruit and take them to town to sell.

One of the most successful watermelon peddlers was a man named Dillon, who used all kinds of tricks to attract buyers to his wagon. Sometimes he hired a banjo player to gather a crowd. Other times he held weight-guessing contests. The person whose guess came closest to the exact weight of the melon won it as a prize. Each Saturday the town folks would pay a visit to Dillon's wagon to see what might be going on.

But one Saturday he made a mistake. That day he held up a forty-pounder and said, "I'll give five dollars to anyone who can eat this melon to the rind, but if he doesn't eat it all, he'll have to pay me a dollar for it."

John, who happened to be standing in the crowd, walked up to the wagon and asked, "Will you give me an hour to decide?"

Mr. Dillon thought it was a strange request, but he agreed, providing, of course, that no one else wanted to try. Well, a forty-pound watermelon is about as big as a small dog or a very large cat, and nobody else was in a mind to try eating it.

It was still there when John returned an hour later and announced he was ready. He cut the melon open and started eating. He went at it like a man who'd been made hungry by a three-day fever, stopping only to catch his breath and spit huge mouthfuls of seeds. Less than ten minutes after he started, all that was left of that forty-pound watermelon was a pile of white and green rind.

Everyone was amazed at this prodigious display of eating—no one more so than Mr. Dillon himself. He had never dreamed he would lose this bet.

"John," he announced, "you won fair and square, and I'm going to give you that five dollars, but before I do I'd like to know why you needed an hour to decide."

"Well," John replied, "it's like this. I knew I had a watermelon at home that was just about the same size, so I went home and ate it. And I figured if I could eat that one, I could eat this one too."

This One
and That One

One chilly, mid-winter day Old Master sent John to town to do a bit of business for him. It was late afternoon before John started back. Frost rimmed the ridges of the road. The sun had already slipped behind the piney woods in the west, and the sky was as black as the bottom of a deep well by the time John passed the cemetery.

Graveyards were places where dead people and ghosts lived, and John didn't want anything to do with those folks. He quickened his pace, but as he walked by the gate he thought he heard someone talking. One part of himself told John to keep on moving as fast as he could, but another part made him creep up closer so he could listen better.

"You take this one and I'll take that one. You take this one and I'll take that one," a voice said.

What John was listening to was two slaves dividing up a sack of sweet potatoes they had liberated from Master's root cellar earlier that day. They figured that since no one ever went to the cemetery after dark, it would be a safe place to split up their bounty.

When John heard the voice say again, "You take this one and I'll take that one," he thought, *Oh my goodness, Judgment Day has come. That must be the Lord and the Devil dividing up everyone's souls.*

Not desiring to be around for such an event, John scooted out of there faster than lightning flashing across the sky. He got back to the plantation without so much as taking a breath, and there was Master waiting for him, as he always was.

"Glad to see you moving so fast, John. That's the way I like you to move. Now, how'd the business go?" he asked.

"Forget that business, Massa. There's more important business going on than your business. The Lord and the Devil are down at the graveyard dividing up souls at this very minute."

"Don't start with your foolishness, John. Just tell me how it went today."

"It ain't foolishness. I'm telling you the truth," said John, glancing over his shoulder to be sure he hadn't been followed. "The Lord and the Devil are down there dividing up souls. I heard it with my own two ears."

"Well, John, why don't we both go down there and have us a look? And if you're lying, I'll have fifty stripes laid across your hide," threatened Master.

"Lay as many stripes as you like, but I'm telling the truth. They're there and they're dividing up souls."

John didn't particularly want to return to the cemetery, but back then white folk did as they pleased, while black folk did as they could, so off he and Master went down the road.

They stood there in the cold, dark night, unable to see anything, when they heard a voice say, "You take this one and I'll take that one. You take this one and I'll take that one."

"Didn't I tell you, Massa? That's them in there, the Lord and the Devil doing their business."

Master thought he heard it right, but it wasn't something he wanted to believe. Besides, it wouldn't do for his slave, any slave, to see he was feeling a little fright.

"Shh," he whispered. "Let's get a little closer."

Just as they reached the gate, the two fellows who'd been dividing the potatoes came to the bottom of the gunnysack. The one who was counting remembered they'd dropped two potatoes as they were entering the cemetery.

"You take these two," he said, "and I'll take the two by the gate."

John and Master didn't waste a single word discussing it. They both started running like two deer trying to get out of the path of a forest fire. They passed each other again and again, but that night for the first time Master ran faster than John, and he was already at the Big House when John arrived.

"Was I right, Massa? Was I right?" gasped John, trying to catch up with his own breath.

Master only nodded his head in agreement (he hadn't caught up with his own breath yet, either) before he went inside. He carefully bolted and locked the door to the night and to anything or anyone who might be out there, but you can be sure it was a long, long time before he doubted John's word again.

$\mathbb{B}$asically there were two kinds of slaves: field hands and house slaves. The field hands did most of the hard, physical labor on the plantation. They plowed the fields, grew the crops, chopped the wood, maintained the roads, and did just about everything else that could weary the bones.

House slaves, on the other hand, had a much easier time of it. They worked in the Big House: cooking, cleaning, polishing, and doing whatever made Old Master and his family more comfortable.

Their labor was clearly different, and generally so were their attitudes. There were even some house slaves who felt closer to their white masters than to their brothers and sisters in common bondage. For example, if their owner came down with an illness, they could be heard to say, "Oh Massa, we're sure feeling sick today, ain't we?" Or if there was some calamity like the barn burning down, they might say, "Oh, ain't it awful that our *barn* burned down?"

Worse still, there were times when some of them for their own benefit would inform on the other slaves.

Who's the Fool Now?

One of the house slaves, George, was always going back to Old Master with stories about the rest of the slaves, stories about who was taking what, about who was only pretending to be too sick to work, all sorts of things no one wanted Master to know about.

Naturally, High John wasn't particularly fond of George, and he decided to teach him a lesson for his tattling ways. One evening he greeted George in the slave quarters. John was smiling that big smile of his and strutting like a rooster stepping in high mud.

"What are you so happy about?" asked George.

"Why, you'll never guess what I did today."

"No, what'd you do today?"

"Why," said John, beaming like a full moon in August, "I cussed out Old Massa."

"You cussed him out?" George asked in surprise. "What'd he do to you?"

"Nothing. He didn't do nothing, and he ain't going to do nothing either. I cussed him out just as much as I pleased. I called him every name a body could think of. I cussed him frontways, backways, sideways, up and down, and you know what, George? He didn't say nothing, and he ain't never going to say nothing."

George turned that over in his mind for a minute or two and said, "Well, the next time he fusses with me I'm going to cuss him out too."

He didn't have to wait long for his chance. The very next day George dropped a tray while he was serving Old Master and Missy a mid-afternoon snack. Master turned on him and started cursing him something terrible. "You stupid, clumsy, no-good—"

But George cut him off in the middle of his anger. "Massa," he said, "you've got no right to talk to me that way. You're no better than a hog wallowing in the mud. You're so dumb that—"

Of course, George didn't get to finish. Master grabbed him by the ear, dragged him out, and gave him a slavery-time whipping. He was in such terrible shape he had to crawl back to the slave quarters, and there was John waiting for him.

"Why George," he said, "what happened to you?"

"What happened to me?" George moaned. "I cussed out Old Massa, and he did this to me. How come he didn't do anything to you?"

"George, you didn't cuss him out to his face, did you?"

"Of course I did. Isn't that what you did?"

"Oh George, what a fool you are," chuckled John. "When I cussed him out, he was up at the Big House and I was way down by the creek. George, some fools' tongues are long enough to cut their throats. You'd best be careful, George. You'd best be careful."

George was very careful after that. It seemed as if he learned his lesson. He even stopped his talebearing, but he didn't forget what John had done to him.

Almost a year had passed when he came whistling and bouncing up to John. "John," he said, "you'll never guess what I did today."

"You didn't go and cuss out Old Massa again, did you?" laughed John.

"No, I didn't do that. I'm not ever going to do that again. What I did was look up Old Missy's dress."

"Hush your mouth," said John. "They'll kill you for even talking like that."

"I don't care. They're not going to do nothing to me. I looked up her dress just as long as I pleased, and let me tell you, John, it sure was sweet."

John tried to put that idea out of his head. It was sure to get him in trouble, but it kept coming back to him again and again. "If a fool like George can get away with that," he thought, "then it should be easy for me."

A few days later, just about the time the sun was dropping behind the trees in the west, John was walking by the Big House. Old Missy was alone on the veranda, sitting in a rocking chair

with her feet up on the railing, sipping a mint julep out of a silver cup.

John couldn't help himself. He crawled up to the edge of the veranda and stuck his head under her starched petticoat. She let out a scream that would have woken up her dead ancestors if they'd been buried within a hundred miles. Old Master came running, and when he saw what had happened, he flew into a rage. He had John tied to a tree and gave him a whipping, both back and front, that would have killed a lesser man.

John couldn't even crawl back to the quarters. He had to be carried. There he lay, bleeding and sweating in the dirt, when George idled up to him and asked, "Why, John, whatever happened to you?"

John could hardly speak. "I peeked up Missy's dress," whispered John, "and Massa nearly whipped me to death. How come he didn't whip you when you did it?"

"You didn't look up her dress while she was in it, did you, John?"

"Yeah," said John. "Isn't that what you told me you did?"

"Oh no," laughed George. "When I looked up

Missy's dress, it was hanging on the clothesline. You know, John, folks say that the price of your hat ain't the measure of your brain, and that's sure true for you. Who's the fool now, John? Who's the fool now?"

George's Dream

◼️ Although George ate pretty well up at the Big House, there were times when he didn't quite fill his belly, and, like the field hands, was forced to use his own ingenuity to get enough to eat.

Early one evening he caught himself a possum and took it on back to his cabin. He set it in a large iron skillet and put coals on the bottom and coals on the top. Then he set potatoes around it and left it to roast all nice and brown. Once it was cooking away, George lay down on his cot and went to sleep. By the time he woke, his lovely dinner would be ready to eat.

Now who should come walking by George's cabin but High John himself. Though he wanted nothing to do with George after their last run-in, and had no intention of stopping, John couldn't help but smell that possum cooking on the coals. "Um-m. That sure does smell good. Why it smells good enough to eat. I think I'll just stop and say hello to my friend, George."

John called out, but George, who was wrapped deeply in his dream about all those victuals, never even heard him. John peeked in the cabin and saw George sleeping. He also saw the skillet, and it didn't take a lot of imagination to guess what was in it.

Very quietly John tiptoed up to that frying pan, whereupon he proceeded to feast upon its contents. He ate everything except for half of one possum leg and a tiny piece of potato. Then he put the possum leg in George's left hand and the potato in his right, and went out as silently as he had come in.

Not long after, George woke from his nap and his dream, thinking about the feast he was about

to partake of. Then he noticed that he was holding a bit of possum and a bit of potato. "Gracious me," he said, "I must've eaten that whole possum already." A few bites and what was left was gone. George sat on the edge of his cot for a few minutes, thinking hard. Then he said, "Yup, I must have eaten it all, but if I did eat that possum and all the taters, they're layin' on my stomach lighter than any meal I've ever had before."

John had done it again, and this time George never even suspected.

The slaves had still another weapon in their struggle for survival. Their owners and the overseers called it "rascality," but it was much closer to out-and-out sabotage—like all those accidents that just seemed to happen.

It only worked, though, if Old Master couldn't prove it, so the slaves often adopted a mask of moving a little slower than they were able, of acting foolish when they weren't, and of not understanding when they did.

They sang about this rascality in a song:

Got one mind for the boss to see.
Got another mind for what I know is me.

And, of course, the master of the fine art of rascality was High John himself.

Deer Hunting

In the pine forests that surrounded many of the farms and plantations there were all kinds of game: rabbits, quail, wild pigs, and deer. Whenever he had time, especially during the winter months when all the cotton was in, Old Master liked to go hunting, and what he liked to hunt most was deer.

One cold day in January, he spotted a huge, twelve-point buck, whose antlers were a good four feet across. Master had never seen a deer like that before, and he wanted it badly. Day after day, he

went into the woods, determined to get that deer.

But that old buck hadn't gotten old by being stupid, so Master was never able to get close enough to get a decent shot at it. Every time he'd see the deer, the deer would see him and run on up the deer trail, always staying far enough ahead to be just out of range.

Old Master figured he might be able to get it with John's help, so one morning he took John hunting with him. "Now, John," he told him, "you wait right here in the middle of this deer trail. I'm going down to the thicket where that big buck likes to stay. I'm going to scare him right up to you. As soon as you see him, start yelling and chase him right back down the trail to me. I'll be coming the other way, and finally I'll have him. Do you understand, John?"

"I sure do, Massa. I sure do. When that deer comes up the trail, I'm just gonna chase him back to you. It'll be as simple as opening my eyes in the morning."

Old Master left John and went down to the thicket. There was the deer. He saw it and it saw him, and just as it always did, the buck started up the trail. It ran right past John, but John simply nodded at it.

A few minutes later, Old Master came huffing and puffing up the trail, barely able to catch his breath. "The deer, John, the deer," he panted. "Where's the deer?"

"Deer? What deer, Massa?" John asked innocently.

"What deer?" screamed Master. "The deer I just chased up the trail. You couldn't help but see him. He came right this way."

"Massa," said John. "I've been standing here just like you told me to, and I ain't seen no deer. The only thing I saw was this fella' go running by wearing a rocking chair on his head. I said 'howdy,' but I guess he was in too much of a hurry to stop."

Old Master knew his slave had done it to him again, but there wasn't much he could do about it. He continued to hunt all through the winter, but from then on he left John home.

Just as the hickories and oaks were beginning to bud out, Master got lucky and managed to kill that deer. It took two shots to do it, though. His first shot hit the hoof of one of the buck's hind legs and slowed it down enough for Master to get close. His second shot went through its head. As a matter of fact, the bullet hit the deer right in the eye.

Since it wouldn't be fitting for a big plantation

owner like himself to drag a deer through the woods, he sent High John to get it. The buck was as heavy as it looked, and John cussed and fussed all the way back to the butchering shed.

Master was waiting when he arrived, and so were two of his friends who'd come for a visit. They admired the buck and Master's hunting skill along with it. Master got all swelled up with pride and began bragging about what a fine marksman he was. "He was moving like a flash of lightning, but I dropped him with a single shot."

One of his friends took a closer look and noticed both bullet holes. Of course, some doubts immediately arose about the possibility of a single shot being the cause of both holes. Master, knowing that John wouldn't dare to disagree with him in front of his friends, called upon him to verify the story, which John did without hesitation.

They asked him directly how one bullet could make two holes. John paused for a moment and said, "Well, you see, that there deer stopped to brush a fly off his eye with his hind foot, and that's when Massa shot him. I guess the bullet must've gone right through his foot and into his eye."

After the visitors left, John said to Old Master,

"I don't mind lying for you if you can't do it for yourself, but next time I'd be mighty grateful if you didn't put the holes so far apart. It took me a whole lot of doing to bring them together."

John's Memory

At different times and different places, High John made himself useful in a number of ways. Of course, he only did so if it would get him out of hard labor.

On one particular plantation, a very large one, John avoided having to go to the fields by becoming the record-keeper.

He told Old Master that keeping all those facts and figures in his head was more than enough work for any man. And further, he said, "If I sweat too much, some of those numbers might just come rolling out with the water."

John was so skillful as a record-keeper that Master came to depend on him and never asked him to do anything else.

One day, though, the Devil appeared and said he wanted to take John.

"Why do you want him?" Master asked.

"Well," replied the Devil, "it's just his time."

"Please, Devil, don't take John," pleaded Master. "He's too important to me. Take anyone else but not John."

To the Devil a slave was a slave, and one didn't seem very different from another, so he asked Master what was so special about John.

"I've got so much to do, I don't have time to keep books or records, but John's memory is so good he keeps it all in his head. If I want to know anything about last year's crops, all I have to do is ask John, and he can tell me exactly how many bales of cotton we harvested or how many bushels of corn we got. If I want to know how much seed we bought two years ago, John can tell me just like that."

"Why, in all my travels, I've never heard the like

of it before," said the Devil. "I'll tell you what. I'll test John's memory, and if it's as good as you say it is, I'll spare him. But if it's not, I'll have to take him."

"Fair enough," said Master.

So the Devil went and found High John. He was napping in the shade of a weeping willow tree with his hat covering his face. What John liked to do best was nothing and to do it slowly, and this was his favorite way to pass an afternoon. The Devil gave him a kick to wake him, but John didn't even bother to take the hat off his face to see who it was. He just mumbled, "What do you want?"

"I want to know," said the Devil, "if you like eggs."

"That I do, that I do," said John, and immediately the Devil disappeared.

Master was certainly relieved to see John that evening. He figured John had passed the Devil's test, and that was the end of it.

But two years later the Devil returned. It was a hot summer day, one of those days when even the insects seem to slow down to an amble, and John was sleeping in the shade of the willow tree, just like the last time.

The Devil kicked John awake, and again John continued to lie there with his hat over his face.

This time the Devil said only one word: "How?"

Without a thought John answered, "Fried," and the Devil vanished.

John had truly passed the test, and the Devil never came back to bother him again.

Freedom

■High John had put it over on Old Master so many times in so many ways that Master began to go a little crazy—not crazy like a quail whose young ones have been stolen from the nest, but more like a mockingbird who's left his mind behind in the last tree.

He would walk aimlessly around the plantation chattering to himself. No one could understand what he was prattling on about because his mumblings were filled with anger and frustration and the words kept bumping up against each other, but Old Master knew exactly what he was thinking and feeling. He only wanted John to behave the way he thought a slave should behave: obedient, humble, submissive, and subservient. He'd tried everything from whippings and whompings to chains and confinement, but John's doings just kept outdoing him.

Finally, all Master wanted to do was get John out of his life. He would have shot him if Old Missy hadn't pointed out that by doing so all he'd end up with was one dead body, whereas if he sold him he'd be a few thousand dollars richer. After all, she reminded him, John was strong and healthy and in his prime, and if you could get him to work, he could do more than most other men.

Master saw the wisdom of this, so when he heard that a rice grower from the low country was in town looking to acquire some stout field hands, he went to him and offered John for sale.

"Never been sick a day in his life," said Master. "He can do the work of two or three men, that is if you can get him to do it."

The rice grower, whose face was wrinkled and scarred as if he had been burnt in a fire, said,

"Slaves are slaves, and the only reason they were put on earth is to work for the likes of me. Like it or not, I've got plenty of ways to make sure they do work."

"That may be so," replied Master, "but it's only fair to tell you John has plenty of ways not to. I hate to admit it, but he's got a silver tongue that's so polished he can make you laugh even when you don't want to."

"Is that so? Well, I should tell you that where I come from I'm known as The Mean Man of the Swamps, and I haven't found anything to laugh at since the day I was born. I'll take him."

And just like that John became someone else's property.

John's new home was deep in the southern swamps. Here they grew rice instead of cotton. They felled the giant cypress trees and split them into pickets and posts and rails. The mosquitoes buzzed and bit every minute of every day, and everyone was expected to work from *can* to *can't*— that is from the first light when a man can see until well after the last light when he can't see.

On the first morning there, John's new owner told him, "Today you're going to dig five hundred

feet of new ditches out there in the marsh, and when you're done doing that you're going to split this pile of logs into rails. By the time I'm through with you you're going to believe that Rest thinks you're dead. You understand me?"

"Oh, I understand you, and it's fine by me," said John, "but seeing that I'm new around here, if I can make you laugh, will you give me the day off?"

So he's starting already, thought The Mean Man of the Swamps—but never having been known even to smile, never mind laugh, he was feeling pretty sure of himself. "If you can make me laugh," he grumbled, "not only will I give you the day off, I'll give you your freedom."

John began to look him up and down, toe to head and back again. Then he walked around him a few times, peering into his ears and his nose until finally he just stood there eyeball to eyeball, looking directly into that burned and twisted face.

"What are you looking at?" demanded The Mean Man of the Swamps.

"I was just thinking," said John, "that I'm looking at about the handsomest man I ever did see anywhere, anyplace, anyhow."

Still scowling, John's new master growled back, "I'm sorry I can't say the same about you."

"Oh, you could Massa, you could," said John, grinning from ear to ear. "You could if you were as big a liar as I am."

The Mean Man of the Swamps, just like Old Master before him, couldn't help himself. He grinned back, and before he could stop himself, he was laughing out loud—and that's how High John the Conqueror got his freedom.

In 1865, after four years of civil war, slavery finally came to an end. It had been 246 years since the first slaves were brought to Virginia. Now the almost four million black people who had been living as slaves were free.

Freedom, though, brought its own problems. Most slaves, under threats of severe punishment, had been prohibited from learning to read or write. Few of them had many skills beyond farming. Tens of thousands left the land and headed for new lives in the cities of both the North and South, but most stayed behind.

The land remained in the possession of those who had owned it before Emancipation—the large farmers and plantation owners. However, they no longer had the free labor that slavery had given them, and now they had no money to pay men and women to work in the fields. Crops had to be grown, and the freed slaves needed food and work, so the system called "sharecropping" began.

Old Master vanished, only to be replaced by Old Boss. High John the Conqueror stayed around, of course, because his will and spirit were still needed.

An Epidemic
of Ducks

■ John had been sharecropping a piece of land with Old Boss. Boss would supply the seed, the tools, and whatever else was needed. John would then prepare the land and plant, grow, hoe, harvest, and chop the cotton. After it was sold and the expenses taken out, Boss and John were supposed to share the profits.

It never seemed to work out that way for John, though. Oh, he would grow a fine crop of cotton all right. No one could do more work than John when he wanted to. And he usually got a pretty good price for it, but every time he'd come back from town with the money there'd be Old Boss waiting for him.

"John," he'd say, "it's time to settle up. How much did you get for the cotton?"

"I got a hundred dollars."

Then Old Boss would take out his pencil and a pad of paper and start making little black marks. All the time he'd be talking to himself, so softly John could hardly make out what he was saying. "Let's see, the seed cost such and such, and the hoes cost such and such, and the such and such cost such and such." He'd go on that way for a while and finally announce, "John, I figure you owe me one hundred and eight dollars and eight cents. Why don't you just give me that hundred dollars and we'll call it being settled up."

This went on year after year. John would work the cotton and sell it, but when it came time to settle up John always ended up with the same he had when he started—nothing.

One year John decided that this time it was going to be different. He brought in a bigger crop than ever before, and as he was taking it to town to sell, there was Old Boss waiting to see him off.

"That looks like a fine wagonload of cotton you've got there. What do you think it'll bring?"

"Well, Boss," said John, shaking his head, "it's mighty hard to say, because I hear tell there's an epidemic of ducks this year."

"An epidemic of ducks? What are you talking about, John?"

"I'm talking about an epidemic of ducks, and I hear them ducks are terrible on cotton prices." With that John just rode off into town leaving Boss standing there by the side of the road, wondering what John could be talking about this time.

John sold the cotton for more money than ever before. He went to the store and treated himself to some sugar, some coffee, and a few other victuals and then headed on home.

Sure enough, there was Old Boss waiting for him with his pencil and pad of paper ready.

"It's time to settle up, John," he said. "How'd we make out this year?"

"Oh Boss, you're going to be pleased to hear that I got a better price than I ever did get before, but like I told you, there was this epidemic of ducks."

"John, there you go talking about those ducks again. What does an epidemic of ducks have to do with anything? Just tell me how much you got so we can settle up."

"I sold the cotton for two hundred dollars. I had the money right here in my hand, but before I could blink twice the ducks got it all."

"John, you're driving me crazy with all this talk about ducks."

"I know, Boss, I know, but let me be more particular. First they deducks for the rotten cotton bolls, and then they deducks for their commission. They deducks for taxes. They deducks for the victuals I got. They deducks for this and they deducks for that, and by the time the ducks were through the ducks got it all—so I guess we'll have to wait until next year to settle up."

John rode on to his cabin while Old Boss just stood there with his mouth hanging open trying to figure out what had happened.

John put away his sugar and his coffee and hid the cotton money. He sat down at his table and said to himself, "All Boss ever wants to do is settle up, when all I want is just a little bit of settling down."

In the first years following the Civil War, things were often as difficult for southern whites as they were for the newly freed slaves, and many people, both black and white, began to take things that were not rightfully theirs. So much stealing went on that not a day passed when the local constable didn't bring at least three or four accused thieves before the judge.

John in Court

One day High John was caught stealing red-handed, and he found himself in a courtroom with two white men who'd also been accused of theft. John usually had some sort of excuse ready to roll off that silver tongue of his, but this time he'd been caught so clearly there was nothing he could think of to say.

John was deeply worried, and with good reason. If found guilty, he could be sentenced to hard labor or to a goodly amount of time in jail. He sat there in the courtroom, waiting his turn, desperately trying to come up with something that would keep him out of jail, but all he could think of was a story he had heard recently.

The story was about ole Sis Goose. She was floating across a pond as graceful as a swan when she came close to the cattail patch at its edge. Suddenly Brer Fox grabbed her and said, "I've got you now Sis Goose. I'm going to break your neck and make a fine dinner out of you."

"Wait a minute!" protested Sis Goose. "This is freedom time now, and I've got as much right as you to be here. That's what the law says. Let's go to court and let the judge decide."

That was fine with Brer Fox, so together they went on down to the courthouse. When they got there, Sis Goose saw that the constable was a fox, the lawyers were all foxes, the judge was a fox, and the jury was nothing but foxes.

Sis Goose had her trial, just like the law said she could, but in the end the court decided that it was perfectly all right for Brer Fox to break her neck and eat her.

That was the story, and High John was beginning to feel more and more like Sis Goose. John was never one to run from fire until he saw the smoke, but it did seem like the smoke was getting

closer and closer. He decided just to sit quiet-like and watch what happened when the others went before the judge.

The first man stepped before the bench.

"You've been accused of stealing a cow," said the judge. "How do you plead? Guilty or not guilty?"

"Not guilty," said the defendent. "I've owned that cow ever since it was a little bitty calf."

"Case dismissed," said the judge.

The next man came forward, and the judge said, "You've been accused of stealing a horse. How do you plead? Guilty or not guilty?"

"I'm not guilty, Your Honor. I've owned that horse from the time he was a young colt."

"Case dismissed," said the judge.

Finally it was John's turn.

"John," the judge said, "you've been accused of stealing a wagon. How do you plead? Guilty or not guilty?"

"Not guilty, Your Honor," said John. "I've owned that wagon ever since it was a wheelbarrow."

There was so much laughter in the courtroom no one was ever sure what the judge said, but you can be sure High John never went to jail.

Tops
and Bottoms

■Now that he was a free man and every drop of sweat was his own, High John was able to turn his mind and body one hundred percent to making his own life better and richer and sweeter, and if the rains fell at the right time and the grasshoppers weren't too thick or hungry, John could urge more crops from a piece of ground than anyone else would have dared dream possible.

John would never forget how it had been during slavery time, and he knew that although the laws had changed a lot of things, they didn't necessarily change everyone's heart. So when John saw that Old Boss had let a chunk of prime bottomland lie fallow for two years running, an idea began to form in that crafty mind of his.

He went to Boss and told him he'd like to rent that land that was simply sitting there doing no one but the worms any good.

"Why that's about the strongest piece of ground I own," said Boss. "I've been meaning to put some cotton in, but you know how busy an important man like myself is." Of course, what he really meant was that without slave labor he couldn't afford to pay anyone to do it for him, and he certainly wasn't going to do it himself.

"But," he continued, "I suppose I could rent it to you if we were to go half and half. You get half and I'll get half. Course, you got to take care of everything, all the way down to the seeds themselves. How's that sound to you, John?"

"That's fine by me, just fine," said John. "But what half do you want?"

"What do you mean what half? I just want half of the crop."

"Boss, I understand you want half, but what I'm asking you is what half? Do you want the top half or the bottom half?"

Boss let that penetrate for a moment or two until he appeared to understand the question, and then, still thinking about cotton, he said, "The top half. I'll take the top half of the crop."

"All right, Boss. You take all the tops and I'll take all the bottoms. We got ourselves a deal."

Even before the buds were fully formed on the poplar trees, John was out there plowing and turning the soil, and as soon as it was warm enough he had the seed in the ground. It wasn't long before the fresh, young shoots were pressing through, reaching for the sun, and right there beside them was General Green; that's what folks called all those weeds and grasses that just seemed to grow up of themselves. But John was there too, going up and down those rows hoeing out all the uninvited guests and taking care of everything else that needed taking care of.

Round about the end of June, High John went to Boss and told him, "Partner, we've got ourselves a mighty fine crop. Yes sir, a mighty fine crop, and I'm wanting to know what you're going to do with your half."

Boss was surprised because it was a little early for the cotton to be ready. He went with John to have a look at their crop, and when he saw it he was more than surprised. He was astonished, because there wasn't a single cotton plant in sight. Instead there stood row after row of twining green potato vines.

"Now," said John, "what do you want me to do with your tops? I'm kind of anxious to cut those greens, 'cause I want to get started digging up all my potatoes."

Old Boss stood there and gaped for a while. Then he began to huff and puff, but he couldn't seem to bring forth a single word. Finally he stomped on home, fuming all the way.

But a man can only fume so much, and once Boss stopped fuming he started scheming, so that the next year when winter was about to give up its space to spring and John appeared to ask about renting the bottomland again, Boss was ready for him—or at least he thought he was.

"So, you want to do tops and bottoms again, eh John?" he clucked with the assurance of a hen who's just laid the perfect egg.

"That's right, Boss, that is if it's acceptable to you."

"Oh, it's fine with me, John, but this year I'll

take the bottoms and you take the tops. Just make sure you bring in as good a crop as you did last year."

"I'll try, Boss. I will surely try. Matter of fact," chuckled John, " there ain't no reason in the world we can't do even better this year."

John set out plowing and planting, and when harvest time came you could hear the crop rustling and whispering in the evening breeze from a long way off.

"We did it again, Boss. We did it again," exclaimed John as he showed Boss this year's bounty. "Why, I believe I'll be getting forty, maybe fifty bushels of wheat an acre, and that's going to leave you with a mighty heap of straw, a mighty heap of straw. Now what'd you say you wanted me to do with your share?"

Boss didn't say. He just huffed off, fuming and cussing all the way because John had tricked him again. This time he fumed longer and schemed deeper, so that when John came around to see about renting the field, Boss *knew* he was ready.

"Which half you want this year?" asked John.

"Well, John," said Boss. "You fooled me once and you fooled me twice, but not even you can fool me a third time. This year I've decided that if you want to work the land you have to give me both the tops and the bottoms."

John didn't respond right away. He stood there quietly and closed his eyes. Then he started scratching his head and wrinkling and crinkling his face as if he were squeezing ideas out of his skin.

"The tops and the bottoms!" he finally said. "But Boss, if you get the tops and the bottoms, what'll be left for me?"

"The middles, John, the middles. That'll be your share. Take it or leave it."

"That's going to make it real tough for me, but if it's take it or leave it, I guess I don't have much choice. I'll take it," said John.

I've got him this time, thought Boss. *There's no way he can get the best of me this year.*

It was late in the summer, the days at their hottest, when John brought Boss to have a look at their crop. Boss was so flabbergasted all he could do was stand there and shake like a dry leaf on a winter tree.

You see, High John hadn't planted cotton. He hadn't planted potatoes and he hadn't planted wheat. What he had planted was a huge field of corn, and there it stood, stalk after stalk, six to seven feet tall, each one holding half a dozen or more jumbo ears of corn.

"Well, Boss," laughed John. "You've got yourself a whole heap of stalks and tassels, but for the life of me I can't figure out what you're going to do with them all. Myself, I like the corn best."

Old Boss had lots of words this time, but they tumbled out in such a jumble John couldn't understand a single one. He just watched Boss tromping on home, shaking his fists in the air and cussing and fussing at the sky as if he hated the whole world.

High John the Conqueror didn't ask to rent that land again. He suspected that Boss would never agree to another deal with him. Besides, after three prime crops in a row, John didn't have any further need of Boss's fields, or anyone else's for that matter.

*T*hese tales show something of what life was like during slavery time and the years that followed, but there are some who would have us think differently. They would have us believe that the slaves actually enjoyed being slaves, that they were sorry to see Emancipation come. And although it's true that a few slaves were seduced into believing that their masters' interests were equal to their own, most lived hating the system and those who kept it alive. As an ex-slave from Alabama said, "There is something 'bout being free that makes up for all the hardships. I's been both slave and free and I knows."*

Just in case there might be any doubts left in your mind about how the people who first told these stories felt toward their oppressors, here is one last tale about High John the Conqueror.

* Thomas Johns quoted in B. A. Bodkin, *Lay My Burden Down*.

The Christmas Turkey

■It was the custom of Old Master and his family to have a turkey dinner every Christmas, and it was John's responsibility to get the turkey ready for the oven.

Thinking he might have some fun at John's expense, Master called him to the Big House just before the holiday.

"John," he said, "you know tomorrow is Christmas."

"Yes, I know," responded John.

"And you know," Master continued, "you take care of the turkey every year."

"Yes Massa, I know that too."

"Well, John, I've decided that this year whatever you do to that turkey we're going to do to you."

John went back to his cabin with a worried mind. He knew he had a serious problem. If he cut off the turkey's head, then Master would cut off his head. If he shot the turkey, he himself would be shot. And if he plucked off all its feathers, Master would probably skin him alive.

John spent most of the night tossing and turning, trying to find a way to save himself. Just before the sun rose on Christmas morning, he got a splendid idea.

When John appeared at the Big House, Old Master and his entire family were waiting on the veranda. They were all looking forward to making a fool of him.

But when he showed up he wasn't carrying a dead and plucked bird. This tom turkey was alive and well and gobbling for the whole world to hear, and John was leading it on a long, red string.

"Merry Christmas to you, Massa," said John.

"And Merry Christmas to you, John. Remember now, whatever you do to that turkey we're

going to do to you," laughed Master, and everyone laughed with him.

"Yes Massa," said John.

Just as if he didn't have a care in the world, John led the big bird right to the edge of the veranda. Then he stepped behind it, dropped to his knees, lifted up its tail feathers, and kissed it right on its butt.

No one said a word, but High John stood up, turned his back on Old Master and his family, lifted his own coattails, and said, "Take your time folks. Take your time. I've got all day."

A Note
about the Stories

■All storytellers know that stories change each
time they're told, and so it is with the stories in
this collection. These are my own versions, de-
veloped over more than a decade of telling them
aloud to both children and adults. They are based
on numerous variant texts collected by folklorists
in the first half of this century and on incidents
related directly to me by men and women in Texas,
Louisiana, Florida, Ohio, and California. In every
case my commitment has been to honor the spirit

of the tale and of High John the Conqueror himself.

The sad truth is that I heard very few tales in their entirety, and they were so bawdy as to make their inclusion impossible. Rather, I heard a bit of a story here, a piece of another one someplace else. It's not that High John has been forgotten. It's more that people simply don't take the time to tell and listen to these stories. As the daughter of an ex-slave in Palestine, Texas, told me, "No more lying* around here. No one's got the time, and them that do got the wrong kind of time *and* the wrong kind of lies."

In the winter of 1979 I went to Eatonville, Florida, hoping to learn more about High John. One hundred and one years ago Eatonville had become the first all-black community ever chartered in the United States. It was also where Zora Neale Hurston grew up and where she later collected so many of the John stories she used in her classic, *Mules and Men.*

One afternoon, while sipping a soda pop at the counter in Ward and Williams' Arkansas Bar-

---

* Lying—a common southern expression used to describe storytelling.

beque, I began to inquire about "a fellow named John or High John. Some folks called him High John the Conqueror," I said rather loudly. "I'm told he used to live around here."

The waitress claimed she didn't know anyone by that name. "I've lived here all my life, and I've never heard of him," she said.

"You know," I persisted. "He wouldn't pick cotton and he wouldn't mow hay. He wouldn't take a licking and he wouldn't run away."

From behind me a woman's voice said, "You got it wrong, boy. He wouldn't work for Disney* and he ain't here today."

At last, I thought, *someone who knows all about John.* The woman who'd recited the verse sat alone. She was very tall and very thin, and she had a large, impressive head of bright, white hair. She agreed to let me join her, but when I was seated at her table it was she who asked the first question. How was it, she wanted to know, that "a stranger in these parts and a white man at that" would have heard about High John?

I told her about my studies, my research, my

* Disneyworld is less than ten miles away and has become, not to everyone's liking, the major employer in central Florida.

storytelling, and about my love and respect for this character. Then I asked her if she knew any stories about John.

"Oh, I do. I surely do," she replied.

Having learned long ago that the only way to receive stories is to give them, I suggested she might like to hear me tell a few. Indeed, she would. I began. There was a scraping of chairs being moved across the floor, and in a moment the three other patrons of the cafe had joined us.

I told two, three, four stories. There was laughter all around, and every so often the white-haired woman, who'd said her name was Wilma, would nod with what I took to be a recognition and acknowledgment of the events I was recounting.

When I finished my fourth story, Wilma said, "I remember some of those. They're good ones."

"Thank you," I replied. "Now, how about you telling one?"

"Oh, I couldn't do that."

"But why? You told me you knew some."

"I do, I do," she blurted out. She paused before going on, and then very deliberately she said, "I know them well enough to know them, but I don't know them well enough to tell them."

Even though Wilma never did tell me a tale that afternoon, High John is still alive—but just barely. If no one takes the time to tell his stories, then they (and John along with them) are sure to vanish forever. Now that you've read them, why not get to know a few well enough to share them with someone else? It is the only way to keep these tales alive and pass the gift on.

STEVE SANFIELD
Montezuma Hill, California
Spring 1988

Bibliography

For those of you who would like to read some of the original versions and versions by other writers and storytellers, the following are recommended:

Abrahams, Roger D. *Afro-American Folktales*. New York: Pantheon Books, 1985.

———. *Positively Black*. Englewood Cliffs, N.J.: Prentice-Hall, Inc., 1970.

Anderson, John Q. "Old John and the Master." *Southern Folklore Quarterly* vol. 25, 1961.

Botkin, B. A., ed. *A Treasury of American Folklore*. New York: Crown Publishers, Inc., 1944.

———, ed. *A Treasury of Southern Folklore.* New York: Crown Publishers, Inc. 1944.

Brewer, J. Mason. *American Negro Folklore.* New York: Quadrangle/The New York Times Book Company, 1968.

———. *Humorous Folk Tales of the South Carolina Negro.* Orangeburg: Claflin College, South Carolina Negro Folk Lore Guild, 1945.

———. "John Tales." In *Mexican Border Ballads and Other Lore*, edited by Mody C. Boatright. Texas Folklore Society, no. 21. Austin, 1946.

———. "Juneteenth." In *Tone the Bell Easy*, edited by J. Frank Dobie. Texas Folklore Society, no. 10. Austin, 1932.

———. *Worser Days and Better Times.* Chicago: Quadrangle Books, 1965.

Courlander, Harold. *Terrapin's Pot of Sense.* New York: Holt, Rinehart and Winston, 1957.

———. *A Treasury of Afro-American Folklore.* New York: Crown Publishers, Inc., 1976.

Dance, Daryl Cumber. *Shuckin' and Jivin': Folklore from Contemporary Black America.* Bloomington: Indiana University Press, 1978.

Dorson, Richard M. *American Negro Folktales.* Greenwich, Conn.: Fawcett Publications, Inc., 1967.

Dundes, Alan, ed. *Mother Wit from the Laughing Barrel: Readings in the Interpretation of Afro-American Folklore.* Englewood Cliffs, N.J.: Prentice-Hall, Inc., 1973.

Eddins, A. W. "From the Brazos Bottoms." In *Texas Folk*

and Folklore, edited by Mody C. Boatright, William M. Hudson, and Allen Maxwell. Texas Folklore Society, no. 26. Austin, 1954.

Fauset, Arthur Huff. "Negro Folk Tales from the South (Alabama, Mississippi, Louisiana)." *Journal of American Folklore*, vol. 40, 1927.

———. "Tales and Riddles Collected in Philadelphia." *Journal of American Folklore*, vol. 41, 1928.

Hamilton, Virginia. *The People Could Fly: American Black Folktales*. New York: Alfred A. Knopf, Inc., 1985.

Hughes, Langston, and Arna W. Bontemps, eds. *The Book of Negro Folklore*. New York: Dodd, Mead and Company, 1958.

Hurston, Zora Neale. "High John the Conqueror." *The American Mercury Magazine*, October 1943.

———. *Mules and Men*. Philadelphia: J. P. Lippincott Company, 1935. Reprint. Bloomington: Indiana University Press, 1978.

Jones, Charles C. *Negro Myths from the Georgia Coast, Told in the Vernacular*. Boston: Houghton, Mifflin and Company, 1888. Reprint. Detroit: Singing Tree Press, 1969.

Kennedy, Stetson. *Palmetto Country*. New York: Duell, Sloan and Pierce, Inc., 1942.

Lester, Julius. *Black Folktales*. New York: Grove Press, 1970.

Oster, Harry. "Negro Humor: John and Old Master." *Journal of the Folklife Institute*, vol. 5, 1968.

Parsons, Elsie Crews. *Folk-Lore of the Sea Islands, South*

Carolina. American Folklore Society, vol. 16. Cambridge, Mass. and New York, 1923. Reprint. Chicago: Afro-American Press, 1969.

Smith, Richard. "Richard's Tales." In *Folk Travelers: Ballads, Tales, and Talk*, edited by Mody C. Boatwright, William M. Hudson, and Allen Maxwell. Texas Folklore Society, no. 25, Austin, 1953.

Spalding, Henry D., ed. *Encyclopedia of Black Folklore and Humor.* Middle Village, N. Y.: Jonathan David Publishers, 1972.

Sterling, Philip, ed., *Laughing on the Outside: The Intelligent White Reader's Guide to Negro Tales and Humor.* New York: Grosset and Dunlap, 1956.

Williams, Girlene Marie. *"Negro Stories from the Colorado Valley."* In *and horns on the toads*, edited by Mody C. Boatwright, William M. Hudson, and Allen Maxwell. Texas Folklore Society, vol. 29. Austin, 1959.

Books about slavery and the slave experience:

Blassingame, John W. *The Slave Community: Plantation Life in the Antebellum South.* New York: Oxford University Press, 1972.

Botkin, B. A., ed. *Lay My Burden Down: A Folk History of Slavery.* Chicago: University of Chicago Press, 1945.

Killion, Ronald, and Charles Waller, eds. *Slavery Time When I Was Chillun Down on Marster's Plantation:*

Interviews with Georgia Slaves. Savannah, Ga.: The Beehive Press, 1973.

Lester, Julius. *To Be a Slave*. New York: The Dial Press, Inc., 1968.

Meltzer, Milton, ed. *In Their Own Words: A History of the American Negro*. New York: Thomas Y. Crowell Company, 1967.

————. *Slavery II*. Chicago: Henry Regnery Company, 1972.

Mullin, Michael, ed. *American Negro Slavery: A Documentary History*. Columbia: University of South Carolina Press, 1976.

Osofsky, Gilbert, ed. *Puttin' on Ole Massa: The Slave Narratives of Henry Bibb, William Wells Brown, and Solomen Morthup*. New York: Harper and Row, 1969.

Stampp, Kenneth M. *The Peculiar Institution: Slavery in the Ante-Bellum South*. New York: Alfred A. Knopf, Inc., 1956.